WELCOME TO
PASSPORT TO READING
A beginning reader's ticket to a brand-new world!

Every book in this program is designed to build read-along and read-alone skills, level by level, through engaging and enriching stories. As the reader turns each page, he or she will become more confident with new vocabulary, sight words, and comprehension.

These PASSPORT TO READING levels will help you choose the perfect book for every reader.

READING TOGETHER
Read short words in simple sentence structures together to begin a reader's journey.

READING OUT LOUD
Encourage developing readers to sound out words in more complex stories with simple vocabulary.

READING INDEPENDENTLY
Newly independent readers gain confidence reading more complex sentences with higher word counts.

READY TO READ MORE
Readers prepare for chapter books with fewer illustrations and longer paragraphs.

This book features sight words from the educator-supported Dolch Sight Words List. This encourages the reader to recognize commonly used vocabulary words, increasing reading speed and fluency.

For more information, please visit passporttoreadingbooks.com.

Enjoy the journey!

Little, Brown and Company

Hachette Book Group
1290 Avenue of the Americas, New York, NY 10104
Visit us at lb-kids.com
everafterhigh.com

Little, Brown and Company is a division of Hachette Book Group, Inc.
The Little, Brown name and logo are trademarks of
Hachette Book Group, Inc.
The publisher is not responsible for websites (or their content)
that are not owned by the publisher.

First Edition: November 2016

ISBN 978-0-316-35678-7

Library of Congress Control Number: 2016943586

10 9 8 7 6 5 4 3 2 1

CW

Printed in the United States of America

Green Light Readers
For the reader who's ready to GO!

"A must-have for any family with a beginning reader."—*Boston Sunday Herald*

"You can't go wrong with adding several copies of these terrific books to your beginning-to-read collection."—*School Library Journal*

"A winner for the beginner."—*Booklist*

Five Tips to Help Your Child Become a Great Reader

1. Get involved. Reading aloud to and with your child is just as important as encouraging your child to read independently.

2. Be curious. Ask questions about what your child is reading.

3. Make reading fun. Allow your child to pick books on subjects that interest her or him.

4. Words are everywhere—not just in books. Practice reading signs, packages, and cereal boxes with your child.

5. Set a good example. Make sure your child sees YOU reading.

Why Green Light Readers Is the Best Series for Your New Reader

• Created exclusively for beginning readers by some of the biggest and brightest names in children's books

• Reinforces the reading skills your child is learning in school

• Encourages children to read—and finish—books by themselves

• Offers extra enrichment through fun, age-appropriate activities unique to each story

• Incorporates characteristics of the Reading Recovery program used by educators

• Developed with Harcourt School Publishers and credentialed educational consultants

To Cristina Isabel, who loves Daniel.
With love from Abuelita

—A. F. A.

For information about permission to reproduce selections from this book, please
write to Permissions, Houghton Mifflin
Harcourt Publishing Company, 215 Park Avenue
South, NY, NY 10003.

www.hmhco.com

First Green Light Readers edition 2002
Green Light Readers is a trademark of Harcourt, Inc., registered in the
United States of America and/or other jurisdictions.

The Library of Congress has cataloged an earlier edition as follows:
Ada, Alma Flor.
Daniel's pet/Alma Flor Ada; illustrated by G. Brian Karas.
p. cm.
"Green Light Readers."
Summary: A young boy takes good care of his pet chicken, and
when she is grown up she gives him a surprise.
[1. Chickens—Fiction. 2. Pets—Fiction.] I. Karas, G. Brian, ill. II. Title.
PZ7.A1857Dap 2002
[E]—dc21 2001007732
ISBN 978-0-15-204825-9
ISBN 978-0-15-204865-5 (pb)

SCP 15 14 13 12 11 10
4 5 0 0 5 4 2 4 8 6
Printed in China

Ages 4–6
Grade: 1
Guided Reading Level: F–G
Reading Recovery Level: 10

Meet the Author and Illustrator

Alma Flor Ada has always loved to write about nature. As a child, she spent hours near a river watching plants, insects, birds, and frogs. Now she lives in a small house near a lake, where she still enjoys watching the natural world.

Brian Karas lives near many farms. He thought about the chickens he sees on those farms as he drew the pictures for *Daniel's Pet*.

Use your hatching egg to tell a friend
about Daniel, his pet chicken Jen,
and Jen's new chicks!

3. Cut the other egg in half.

4. Tape one half at the top and the other half at the bottom.

1. Cut out two egg shapes.

2. Draw a chick on one egg.

Hatching an Egg

You can make one of Jen's new baby chicks!

WHAT YOU'LL NEED

- paper
- crayons or markers
- scissors
- tape

Think About It

1. **What is Daniel's pet?**

2. **What does Daniel's pet do?**

3. **Is Daniel surprised? How can you tell?**

4. **Why will Daniel have lots of pets now?**

5. **Would you like to have pets like Daniel's? Why or why not?**

"Oh my!" said Daniel.
"Now I will have lots of pets!"

"Jen is in here," said Mama.
"Look at her eggs."

One day, Daniel didn't see Jen.
"Jen! Jen!" Daniel called.

Jen got very big.

Daniel fed Jen every day.

Daniel fed all the hens.

Daniel fed Jen.

"I'll call her Jen," said Daniel.

"Can I have her as a pet?"
"Yes, Daniel," said Mama.

It was soft in his hands.